W9-ARS-416

This edition published by Parragon Books Ltd in 2016
and distributed by

Parragon Inc.
440 Park Avenue South, 13th Floor
New York, NY 10016
www.parragon.com

Copyright © Parragon Books Ltd 2012–2016

All rights reserved. No part of this publication may be reproduced, stored in a retrieval
system, or transmitted, in any form or by any means, electronic, mechanical, photocopying,
recording, or otherwise, without the prior permission of the copyright holder.

ISBN 978-1-4748-6367-4

Printed in China

THE EMPEROR'S NEW CLOTHES

Retold by
Katherine Sully

Illustrated by
Deborah Allwright

PaRragon

Bath • New York • Cologne • Melbourne • Delhi
Hong Kong • Shenzhen • Singapore

Once there was an emperor who was very proud of how he looked.

More than anything, he loved new clothes. He bought the finest silk and satin, velvet and lace, and he kept the royal tailors busy day and night, making new clothes.

They even made matching outfits for the emperor's little dog.

The royal closets were overflowing!

Every morning, the emperor would admire himself
in the mirror and say,

"Aren't I the best-dressed emperor in the whole wide world?"

No matter what they really thought, everyone around him
would bow and say, "Yes, Your Majesty, you are."

Every year, the emperor led a royal parade through the city, wearing his very best clothes. But one year, he decided that even his best clothes would not do.

"This year," he told his tailors, "I want to wear an outfit so splendid no one will ever forget it!"

The tailors worked day and night making the best clothes they could fashion. They brought the emperor piles and piles of new clothes to try on. But nothing pleased him.

"These clothes are much too ordinary,
I must have something
much **more magnificent!**"

The tailors kept trying, but the emperor was still not happy. At last he told his chief minister, "Find me some new tailors, who can make truly magnificent clothes!"

The chief minister set out at once. As he walked through the marketplace, he overheard two men talking to a well-dressed couple.

"We are the best tailors in the land," the first man was saying.

"Yes," the other agreed. "We make clothes so fine that no one in the whole world has ever seen anything like them!"

The chief minister rushed over.

"You must come with me to the emperor's palace," he told the tailors.

The chief minister brought the two tailors to the emperor.

"Can you make clothes that are truly magnificent?" the emperor asked them.

"Oh, yes, Your Majesty," they replied. "When people see our clothes, they never forget them!"

"What is so special about your clothes?" asked the emperor.

"They are made from a rare and wonderful cloth," the first tailor explained, "and only we know how to weave it."

"That sounds perfect!"

exclaimed the emperor.

He gave the tailors a bag of gold and promised
them more when the clothes were finished.

The two tailors were given their own workshop, where no one would disturb them. They quickly went to work.

A few days later, the chief minister came to see how they were doing. The tailors seemed to be very busy—but the chief minister could not see any cloth.

"Our cloth is very fine and delicate," the first tailor explained. "See how it shimmers in the light."

"Only a fool cannot see this beautiful cloth," said the second tailor.

The chief minister did not want the tailors to think he was a fool, so he said, "Yes, it is very beautiful indeed."

The tailors pretended to snip off a piece of cloth, then carefully fold it up. They handed it to the chief minister, who took it straight to the emperor.

"Only a fool cannot see this wonderful cloth," said the chief minister, handing the invisible cloth to the emperor.

The emperor did not want anyone to think he was a fool, so he quickly said,

"Yes, it is the most beautiful cloth I have ever seen!

Give the tailors more money, and tell them to work more quickly!"

A week later, the chief minister went to see the tailors again.

They seemed to be hard at work, cutting and pinning their invisible cloth.

"What do you think of the cloak we are making?" asked the first tailor.

"Only a fool would not be able to see how beautiful it is!" said the second tailor.

Because he did not want to look like
a fool, the minister replied, "It is the
most splendid cloak I have ever seen. I
am sure the emperor will be pleased!"

At last, the day of the parade arrived. The emperor eagerly went to his dressing room, where the tailors were waiting.

Very carefully, the tailors helped the emperor put on his wonderful new clothes.

Of course, the emperor could not see any clothes at all! But he didn't want the tailors to think he was a fool, so he said,

"These are the most magnificent clothes I have ever worn."

Smiling, he admired himself in the mirror.

Wearing nothing at all, the emperor made his way down the grand staircase, through the great hall, and out to the palace courtyard.

Everyone bowed as the emperor passed. No one noticed that he wasn't wearing any clothes!

The parade made its way through the city.

Crowds of people stood in the streets, cheering and clapping, waiting for the emperor to appear.

When they saw the emperor at last, they could not believe their eyes!

The people began to whisper to one another. But no one had the courage to say anything out loud.

One little boy and his sister made their way to the front of the crowd.

As soon as they saw the emperor, they began to laugh and point at him.

"Look!" they giggled. "The emperor has no clothes on!"

And everyone, even the emperor himself, knew it was true.

Filled with shame, the emperor made
his way back to the palace to get dressed.

"I have been **very** foolish," he said to his chief minister.

"If my appearance had not been so important to me, I would never have let myself be cheated by those two tailors. I will never be so vain about my clothes again."

He was true to his word—and he was a much happier emperor from that day on.

The End